PLEASE LET ME HELP

"HELPFUL" LETTERS TO THE WORLD'S MOST WONDERFUL BRANDS

ZACK STERNWALKER

MICROCOSM PUBLISHING
PORTLAND, ORE

PLEASE LET ME HELP
"Helpful" Letters to the World's Most Wonderful Brands

© Zack Sternwalker, 2002, 2018
This edition © Microcosm Publishing, 2018
First edition, first published 2002
This edition, first published November, 2018

ISBN 978-1-62106-400-8
This is Microcosm #256
Cover by Kelly Fry
Inside covers by Dan Cole | Errant.Graphics
Book design by Joe Biel

For a catalog, write or visit:
Microcosm Publishing
2752 N Williams Ave.
Portland, OR 97227
(503) 799-2698
MicrocosmPublishing.com

To join the ranks of high-class stores that feature Microcosm titles, talk to your local rep: In the U.S. **Como** (Atlantic), **Fujii** (Midwest), **Travelers West** (Pacific), **Brunswick** in Canada, **Turnaround** in Europe, **New South** in Australia and New Zealand, and **Baker & Taylor Publisher Services** in Asia, India, and South Africa.

Global labor conditions are bad, and our roots in industrial Cleveland in the 70s and 80s made us appreciate the need to treat workers right. Therefore, our books are MADE IN THE USA and printed on post-consumer paper.

Library of Congress Cataloging-in-Publication Data

Names: Sternwalker, Zack, author.
Title: Please let me help : very serious letters to the world's most
   wonderful brands / Zack Sternwalker.
Other titles: Letters to the world's most wonderful brands
Description: First edition. | Portland, OR : Microcosm Publishing, 2018.
Identifiers: LCCN 2017061212 | ISBN 9781621064008 (pbk.)
Subjects: LCSH: Divorced men--Fiction. | Entrepreneurs--Fiction. | Meaning
   (Philosophy)--Fiction. | Psychological fiction. | GSAFD: Epistolary
   fiction. | Humorous fiction.
Classification: LCC PS3619.T478745 P54 2018 | DDC 813/.6--dc23
LC record available at https://lccn.loc.gov/2017061212

MICROCOSM · PUBLISHING

Microcosm Publishing is Portland's most diversified publishing house and distributor with a focus on the colorful, authentic, and empowering. Our books and zines have put your power in your hands since 1996, equipping readers to make positive changes in their lives and in the world around them. Microcosm emphasizes skill-building, showing hidden histories, and fostering creativity through challenging conventional publishing wisdom with books and bookettes about DIY skills, food, bicycling, gender, self-care, and social justice. What was once a distro and record label was started by Joe Biel in his bedroom and has become among the oldest independent publishing houses in Portland, OR. We are a politically moderate, centrist publisher in a world that has inched to the right for the past 80 years.

Zack Sternwalker
P.O. Box #22883
Oakland, CA 94609

Microcosm Publishing
2752 N Williams Ave
Portland, OR 97227

DEAR MICROCOSM PUBLISHING,

I'd like to begin by congratulating you on appearing on the 47th page of a Google search for "best publishers." While this may seem like you were really far down the line in the search, you'll be pleased to know that there were a great many more pages of publishers. Besides, I think the number 47 is kind of a lucky number (it sort of looks like someone hiccupped while trying to draw a swastika).

I'll admit that after your name came up so far down the line in the Google search, I was a bit skeptical, but after looking at your website and seeing how well you'd organized all your books into specific categories, I knew I was in the right place. Which brings me to the point of this letter.

I believe that I've created a new book category—or rather, a new literary form, and I'd like for your publishing company to help introduce it to the public. Please allow me to recount the origin of its discovery.

The other night my mom and I were in our living room, painting cardboard boxes to look like dogs. I've been contracted (loosely) to shoot a stop motion animation documentary for the local SPCA about Abraham Lincoln's childhood dog, Chamomile.

While I was arranging the "dogs" around the waterfall (my mom's curtains), I realized I was one dog short. I asked my mom to grab another cardboard box from the area of the living room where we keep them, but to my surprise she said we were all out.

Now I know what you're thinking: "Why didn't you just go to the store and buy another cardboard box?" Well, for starters, I never do that. Secondly, I had scripted these particular dogs to be the elders of the community, and I wanted them to have that weathered, seen-it-all look, which could never have been achieved with a brand new cardboard box.

With that in mind, I hurried up to the attic. After crawling around a bit, I spotted a smallish, dusty one tucked back beneath an old salamander costume. I dragged it out, carried it downstairs, and dumped out its contents on the floor.

Imagine my surprise when thousands of old letters spilled across the carpet. As I knelt down and started reading them, it all came flooding back to me. Allow me to explain.

Twelve years ago my life was very different. For starters, I lost my job and was forced (with only several years' warning) to move out of my then living situation and back into my childhood home. While this was jarring in some ways, it also afforded me a cleared mental space to reflect, refine, and begin again.

Because I was having trouble finding work, I decided to spend my time coming up with inventions and doing what I really love: writing screenplays for my favorite actors.

And because I had nothing to lose, I decided to write letters to the people and companies I hoped to collaborate with in the hopes that we could work together. While many of the people I contacted wrote back (ecstatically), others seemed too busy to reply.

As I read over these letters again in my living room with my mom, twelve years later, I was surprised that in addition to all the interesting ideas, a strange picture of myself was also being painted, almost by accident.

Equally compelling was the way in which the people and companies I wrote followed suit: slowly revealing small pieces of their lives and growing more comfortable with me sentence by sentence. (I found it very interesting how their letters often began with a very formal "Dear Zack," only to end with an emotionally charged, "Sincerely.")

This unique aspect to the correspondence was so interesting that I suddenly caught myself saying out loud, "It's almost like these letters are doing something never previously done, something in which a correspondence becomes something deeper." I tried to think of a fitting literary term, but nothing came to mind.

That's when my mouth blurted out the word "correspondation."

Correspondation? I closed my eyes and said it again, this time while envisioning a flock of doves being let out of an enclosure. Which brings me to the point of this letter.

I would like for your publishing company to help me introduce this new literary term, via this collection of letters from twelve years ago. Naturally a strong title is a first step, so you'll be pleased to know I've already come up with several. Working titles are: *Allow Me to Help, Actors and Companies I Wrote*, and *Is It Okay If I Help You Out?*

In addition to a cutting edge literary product, if you decide to work with me on this project you'll also have the wisdom of a seasoned screenwriter at your beck and call. To advertise for the book—and because I already have a substantial collection of cardboard boxes painted as dogs—I thought we could film a series of short commercials in which the "dogs" walk around the local library searching for the correspondation section, only to constantly be disappointed (we can show their displeasure by having them pee on the other books). And don't worry about how we can get fake pee, I can either save up real pee (me and my mom's) or let a yellow marker soak overnight in some dog pee.

If you are interested in working with me on this project (which I hope you are), please contact me as soon as possible.

ZACK STERNWALKER

P.S. As a sign of good faith, please accept this complimentary vampire.

Zack Sternwalker
P.O. Box #22883
Oakland, CA 94609

Justin Timberlake
P.O. Box 1070
Windermere, FL 34786

DEAR JUSTIN TIMBERLAKE,

Let me be the first to congratulate you on the outstanding quality of your 2002 album, *Justified*. I just bought it yesterday and have already listened to it from start to finish. My favorite song is "Let's Take a Ride," because it fully captures the emotional struggle of being a single father in the rainy city of Seattle (it's hard to sleep when you miss your dead wife).

However, despite the album's strengths (and there are too many to count), I couldn't help noticing that you chose to exclude the oboe as a featured instrument. I believe this was a serious mistake—most likely the result of an inexperienced producer.

Now it just so happens that I've recently become unemployed and suffered through a bitter divorce. Instead of complaining (turn that frown upside down), I've used the free time to brush up on my oboe-playing (I was second chair in my high school band).

Of course I realize it's too late to add an oboe track to your most recent album (that would be crazy), but I'd like to offer my services and help with your next one.

I know you may be a bit skeptical of my ability on the instrument, so let me put those fears to rest. Not only am I familiar with such popular classics as "Jingle Bell Rock" and "When Johnny Comes Marching Home," but I've also written several compositions of my own, complete with lyrics that I envision you singing. Some of the song titles are: "Oboe on My Knee," "Oh Boy, Oboe!," "Sleep Like an Oboe," and "Oboe Lobo" (a ballad in Spanish).

I have a good four-track, several working microphones, and my bedroom is reasonably noise proof. If it works for you, why don't you come by the house (I hope you like cats) sometime in the evening. That way we can lay down a few tracks and then order a pizza or something.

Also, I've heard that spicy foods can damage vocal cords, so when you go to Taco Bell be sure to put the mild sauce on your burrito (save the heat for our songs).

Please contact me with your schedule of availability. I hope to hear from you soon.

ZACK STERNWALKER

P.S. As a sign of good faith, please accept this complimentary vampire.

Zack Sternwalker
P.O. Box #22883
Oakland, CA 94609

Canadian Embassy
501 Pennsylvania Ave, NW
Washington, DC 20001

DEAR CANADA,

Let me begin by saying how much I admire your country. From what I've heard, you have a lot of pretty nature and people who speak French.

That being said, I'm having trouble understanding your decision to invade the Middle East.

I know the opinion of someone like myself, raised in a country without a history of war, may not count for much, but I just can't grasp your reasoning. Did you really think Saddam Hussein had weapons of mass destruction? Do you know how many people die from a war?

But I'm not angry with you. In fact, I would like to represent you globally.

In a stroke of good fortune, I've recently become unemployed and thus can offer my full service to you. I'm a good public speaker and even know a bit of Spanish (Canada no es malo). I also have the ability to reason with those Americans who may be harboring certain prejudices against your ruthless, war-driven country.

Additionally, I will soon have solid connections with top players in the entertainment industry who can aid in numerous pro-Canada movie endeavors. Some working titles are: *AIDS Doesn't Come from Canada, Canadians Discovered the Sun,* and *Ghandi: The Story of a Canadian Farm Boy.* The latter of the three focuses on a young Ghandi as he struggles to break free from his overbearing father and follow his dream of starting an all-oboe pop band. The climax of the film occurs when Ghandi plays his oboe in the middle of an abandoned parking lot and stalks of corn slowly rise up through the cement.

If you are interested in employing me, I think it would be worthwhile to give me a crash course in Canadian culture so I could better incorporate it into my projects. Please send one airline ticket to the above address plus some spending money for the airport (I need my *People* magazine).

I look forward to working with your government to better educate the global community. Hope to hear from you soon.

ZACK STERNWALKER

P.S. As a sign of good faith, please accept this complimentary vampire.

Zack Sternwalker
P.O. Box #22883
Oakland, CA 94609

U.S. Service Center
Citi Inquiries
100 Citibank Drive
P.O. Box #769004
San Antonio, TX 78245-9004

DEAR CITIBANK,

Let me begin by saying how much I enjoyed banking with you. Your customer service was excellent and your ATMs were conveniently located near all my favorite restaurants, bars, and shopping destinations.

Although I'm not currently banking with you, that's more to do with my lack of steady employment, which brings me to the point of this letter.

Recently I've been renting a lot of old western movies and have noticed how frequently banks are the selected targets for robberies. It seems like a fairly easy task if you can get a revolver, a bandana (to obscure your identity), and a fast horse.

As such, my first suggestion to your company would be to forbid the parking of horses anywhere near your banks.

Next, I think it would be a good idea to keep a substantial amount of the money in a secret location away from the bank itself. As I mentioned above, I've recently become unemployed and have been forced to move back in with my mother. Although her house is quite small, my bedroom is really big. I'm not an accountant, but from taking a few crude measurements I think it could hold a lot of money (this excludes a small corner of the room set aside for dance practice).

Now I realize that a bank can't function without some money on hand, so this is my proposal.

I'll come by next Tuesday with my mom's car (it'd have to be in the morning because I have an afternoon commitment) and fill it up with all the money that usually sits in the big safe. I'll take the money home to my room (I have a lock on my door, so don't worry) and keep an eye on it. That way if the bank were to be robbed it would only lose a small amount of its actual funds.

And if, by some rare act of God, a robber did break into my mom's house trying to get your money, I still have my old Louisville Slugger baseball bat from when I played little league. This, coupled with my knowledge of the human body's many debilitating locations, makes me a serious threat to any would-be intruder.

As a last resort, I will carry a small whistle in my pocket so that if I get into trouble I can just blow it and my mom will come running.

Sometime next week I'd like to come by and take a look at how much money you want me to take so I can set aside the appropriate number of trash bags for its transport.

Hope to hear from you soon.

ZACK STERNWALKER

P.S. As a sign of good faith, please accept this complimentary vampire.

Zack Sternwalker
P.O. Box #22883
Oakland, CA 94609

Harley-Davidson Customer Service
3700 W. Juneau Avenue
Milwaukee, WI 53208

DEAR HARLEY-DAVIDSON,

Let me be the first to congratulate you on firmly establishing yourself as one of the premier motorcycle manufacturing companies in the world. From what I've heard your motorcycles adhere to the quality standards established for motorcycles.

Despite this accomplishment, I wonder if anyone in your company has heard about the new environmentally safe vehicles being built.

While I'm not implying that your motorcycles are the reason for our damaged ozone layer, I am merely suggesting that your company could yet tap into this lucrative consumer trend.

By now you are probably asking yourselves, "How would we build the first environmentally safe motorcycle?"

Well, that is where I come in. I've recently become unemployed and have used this time to invent the first engine-free motorcycle, which I call *The Pedaler*.

I'm not going to give away the entire design (my lawyer friend says I should be careful), but I will tell you the basic idea. Instead of a normal gas-guzzling motorcycle engine, *The Pedaler* is powered entirely by the rider. In fact, its name comes from the pedaling action which causes the rear wheel to revolve.

Since I designed it, I feel that I am the most qualified to envision the various commercials that could introduce this revolutionary machine to the public. In my opinion the best ad campaigns are the ones that really make the viewer think. With this in mind, please allow me to give you a brief plot treatment.

The commercial opens on a formal dinner party. Guests are dressed in their best attire. They engage in small talk and compliment the excellent cuisine.

Then the host taps his glass and proposes a toast. Everyone raises their drinks as he thanks them for coming. Then he announces that he has recently married and would like to take this opportunity to introduce everyone to his new bride, who has just flown in from the Czech Republic. He removes a small hand bell from his pocket and rings it.

Suddenly the kitchen door bursts open and two monkeys atop *The Pedaler* ride in. The guests scream as the monkeys ram *The Pedaler* into the host and then jump onto his face, scratching and biting him.

When the monkeys finally scurry out of the room, the host turns apologetically to his guests and says, "At least she's environmentally safe."

Although I'd prefer *The Pedaler* be introduced by the Harley-Davidson company, it's only fair to tell you that I've written a similar letter to the Honda Corporation. I imagine it will take them longer to get back to me because of the language barrier, but I wouldn't hold off for too long if I were you.

Hope to hear from you soon.

ZACK STERNWALKER

P.S. As a sign of good faith, please accept this complimentary vampire.

Harley-Davidson Motor Company, 3700 West Juneau Ave., PO Box 653, Milwaukee, WI 53201

November 10

Zack Sternwalker
P O Box 22883
Oakland, CA 94609

Dear Zack Sternwalker:

Thank you for taking the time to write. We appreciate your enthusiasm for Harley-Davidson. However, our One-Hundred-plus years of experience have taught us the pitfalls of accepting unsolicited ideas, no matter how good or well intentioned.

Like most successful companies, we have had too many instances of people claiming that they gave us ideas and are entitled to compensation. As you can imagine, it is impossible to determine in advance those who are trying to take advantage of us. In addition, we receive very few ideas that have not already been suggested by our employees, suppliers and vendors.

For these reasons, we have adopted a policy of accepting product or promotional ideas only when submitted with a properly completed "Submitting Ideas to Harley-Davidson Motor Company" form.

Although this is probably not the response that you anticipated, I hope that it does not reduce your enthusiasm for Harley-Davidson or for motorcycling.

Thanks again for taking the time to write.

Sincerely,

Kathie Grzelak
Harley-Davidson Customer Service
231033

Zack Sternwalker
P.O. Box #22883
Oakland, CA 94609

Church of Jesus Christ of Latter-day Saints
15 East South Temple
Salt Lake City, UT 84150

DEAR CHURCH OF JESUS CHRIST OF LATTER-DAY SAINTS,

I'd like to begin by saying how much I enjoy your religion. I wasn't raised a Mormon but was recently invited to a service and was quite impressed.

However, I was a little disappointed to learn that there isn't one really large Mormon temple to which people can make a pilgrimage. Big, decadent churches are already an incentive to join most religions, so they could also do wonders for yours.

Allow me to help out with this project.

First off, we must decide on a location. I'm thinking somewhere in Alaska because that state already has a certain mysticism about it. Just think: in the future it could be every person's dream to visit the Mormon temple of gold in the mystical land of Alaska—which brings me to my next suggestion.

The temple should be made entirely of gold.

Also it should be built in the shape of a giant number seven.

I've recently become unemployed, and since it is my idea I would like to be the head contractor on the project. I took two years of wood shop in junior high and received straight Bs, so it wouldn't be my first time around construction.

Moreover I'm good at motivating large groups of people. After we construct the golden seven I estimate it'll take at least a hundred men to lift it upright using ropes. I feel entirely qualified to yell, "Now!" or "Hoist!" in such a way that the men will understand that we are building a house of God and give it one hundred and ten percent.

Since this is such an important project I think it'd only be fair to document it cinematically. We could film it in a rough and tumble documentary style, focusing on the daily interactions of the men as they work, eat lunch, and part ways at the end of the day.

If you're into the idea, we could also edit in footage of the men being quizzed on their knowledge of the Mormon religion (they might not know as much as you think).

Of course with any construction project there are bound to be accidents that result in serious injury or even death. With a live camera crew present we'll be able to capture these dramatic moments as they unfold before our very eyes (if someone does die, at least their loved ones can take solace in the fact that it made a fantastic scene).

Working titles for the documentary are: *Raise the Golden Temple*, *A Perfect Place to Pray*, and *Even Wild Bears Need Honey*.

If at all possible, I'd like one of your representatives to come by my house next week and look over some rough architectural sketches I've drawn. Please contact me with your schedule of availability.

I hope to hear from you soon.   ZACK STERNWALKER

P.S. As a sign of good faith, please accept this complimentary vampire.

Zack Sternwalker
P.O. Box #22883
Oakland, CA 94609

Francis Ford Coppola
916 Kearny St.
San Francisco, CA 94113

DEAR FRANCIS FORD COPPOLA,

Let me begin by saying that you are an incredible director. My favorite movie of yours is *Sleepless in Seattle* because it made me think of Seattle and how much it rains there (I bet you had to wear some real big galoshes during production).

Anyway, I've recently become unemployed and have been forced to move back in with my mother. The other day I was watching *Extra* (a popular news program that focuses on the entertainment industry) and saw that you have a daughter. All this time I thought you were just a movie director, but it looks like you also put aside a little time for the old you-know-what.

Now I'm sure the strain of a new baby is making it quite hard for you to focus on your next film. I remember when my son was born things were so hectic I could hardly arrange for my divorce proceedings, which is the reason why I've contacted you.

I would like to offer you my full babysitting services.

Allow me to describe the start of a sample evening.

I arrive promptly at eight just as you and the wife are off to your important Hollywood soiree. You don't smell alcohol on my breath. I'm freshly bathed. I'm wearing a little orange hat that makes babies laugh. I've even memorized the emergency phone number for the police, fire, and ambulatory services.

If by some rare chance little Sofia begins to cry I can even provide high quality live entertainment in the form of my unique puppet shows.

So what's the all-time best subject matter for a puppet show?

Swimming pools. But don't worry, this isn't just some cliché swimming pool story. This is the story about that one swimming pool who's allergic to chlorine.

Allow me to give you a brief plot treatment.

The story begins on the day all the little swimming pools are lining up to get their first dose of chlorine. Everyone is excited and talking about how it will feel to finally have chlorine in their water.

However, when our own pool receives the chlorine it suddenly falls to the ground and goes into convulsions. Terrified of being rejected by its peers, it runs away in search of a new life purpose.

Eventually it discovers malt liquor and spends the rest of the story intoxicated.

Working titles are: *One More for the Road*, *Drink It Up Drink It Down*, or *The Shallowest End*.

I have the highest standards for the kind of entertainment that the children of today are exposed to, and I feel that having me around, as well as my unique puppet shows, could only be an asset to your daughter's growth (creativity needs to be nurtured at her tender age).

With this in mind, I'd like to invite you and little Sofia by for a quick meet-and-greet session sometime towards the end of next week. Please contact me with your schedule of availability.

Hope to hear from you soon.   ZACK STERNWALKER

P.S. As a sign of good faith, please accept this complimentary vampire.

Zack Sternwalker
P.O. Box #22883
Oakland, CA 94609

The Coca-Cola Company
Attn: Good Answer
P.O. Box #1734
Atlanta, GA 30301

DEAR COCA-COLA COMPANY,

On a recent visit to my local grocer, I noticed the addition of your complete line of beverage products to the supermarket's shelves. Let me be the first to congratulate you on this amazing accomplishment.

But despite this wonderful success (you have every reason to be proud), I couldn't help but notice the absence of a lemonade-style beverage, and this confuses me immensely.

I love lemonade and so does my mom. In fact, most people I've met (and I've met a great deal of people) also love lemonade. Failing to corner the lemonade soda market is a grave mistake on the part of any beverage manufacturer, so you'll be glad to hear I'm willing to help you be the first company to make lemonade soda (or *Lemondoda*) a household name.

So what will be my role? Well, I happen to know several places to get lemons. I also know precisely how much water and sugar to add. Moreover, I've recently become unemployed and have plenty of time on my hands.

Here is my proposal: Every Tuesday (my mom lets me have the car for the whole afternoon) I'll bring down a few barrels of my homemade lemonade to your manufacturing plant and your employees can do the necessary canning, carbonating, and labeling.

Also, a good portion of why I choose to drink a certain beverage has to do with the engaging commercial spots. I would like to help in this arena as well.

Allow me to give you a brief plot treatment of my best idea.

To introduce the new product, I envision a scene of a young man walking casually down the street. He's smiling, possibly clutching a tennis racket.

Suddenly a car drives by and guns him down. We see in slow motion as each bullet pierces his body, splattering blood on the passersby.

Our character falls to the ground and a young woman runs from the crowd. She crouches besides him and begins to stroke his forehead and hum the popular Justin Timberlake song "Let's Take a Ride." She leans in and asks if he'll make it and we pan to a close-up of his lips, obviously parched from thirst.

He reaches up and touches her cheek and whispers, "I'll live . . . for *Lemondoda*."

I would like to invite your representatives over sometime next week to try my lemonade and decide on some appropriate directors for the project.

ZACK STERNWALKER

Hope to hear from you soon.
P.S. As a sign of good faith, please accept this complimentary vampire.

November 12

Mr. Zack Sternwalker
P.O. Box 22883
Oakland, CA 94609

Dear Mr. Sternwalker:

Thank you for contacting us at The Coca-Cola Company. We appreciate your interest in our Company.

Because of our worldwide visibility, we receive many unsolicited suggestions from persons outside of our Company. We are complimented that our consumers are interested enough in our Company to want to help us improve our performance. At the same time, however, we are unable to consider any submissions from persons or business groups outside the Company when the submission relates to advertising, sales promotions, formula modifications for any of our brands, or concepts we have previously reviewed.

Thank you again for contacting us.

Sincerely,

INDUSTRY AND CONSUMER AFFAIRS
THE COCA-COLA COMPANY

Zack Sternwalker
P.O. Box #22883
Oakland, CA 94609

Jerry Bruckheimer
c/o Staff Member Creative Artists Agency LCC (CAA-LA)
9830 Wilshire Blvd. Beverly Hills, CA 90212

DEAR JERRY BRUCKHEIMER,

Let me begin by saying that I'm one of your biggest fans. I see a lot of movies and never hesitate to tell people that the ones you produce are the very best. My favorite is *Sleepless in Seattle* because it made me want to go to Seattle and to be an insomniac.

Now I know it's been a while since you've done something so I'd like to propose a project that could help jump-start both our careers.

Recently I've gone through a bitter divorce, become unemployed, and been forced to move back in with my mother. Fortunately I've used this time to focus on my screenwriting.

In the last few months I've written a beautiful script about that terrible bombing in Pearl Harbor (I was amazed to find that no movie has ever been made dealing with this horrific event). Moreover, I think a film of this type is very timely what with all the trouble between Canada and foreign countries (if they want to go to war, we might as well cash in).

Allow me to give you a brief plot treatment.

The film begins shortly after the bombing (no costly explosions). Our main character has lost his arms and legs and is forced to move in with his estranged sister who is a well-known porn actress specializing in bestiality.

Home life is tense between the two until one climactic night when the sister brings home an adorable puppy. I don't want to give it all away but let's just say there's a very moving shower scene involving our disabled hero, the puppy, and a whole lot of aluminum foil.

Working titles are: *Harboring the Pearl*, *Last Pearl in the Harbor of Ill Refute*, and *Sibling Sluts: On the Floor and Against the Door*.

I would've liked Tom Cruise to play the lead but he's already working with me on another project and I wouldn't want him overloaded. As a second choice I would take Sidney Poitier as long as he agrees to have actual intercourse in the film's numerous, explicit sex scenes (realism is crucial).

If you're available next week, I'd like to invite you over for dinner so we can talk over the project, face to face. Contact me with your schedule of availability.

I hope to hear from you soon.

ZACK STERNWALKER

P.S. As a sign of good faith, please accept this complimentary vampire.

November 18

Zack Sternwalker
P.O. Box #22883
Oakland, CA 94609

This is with reference to your letter regarding your screenplay.

Because so many unfounded claims of plagiarism are asserted against motion picture producers, this company has made it an invariable rule that neither it nor its employees read or consider unsolicited literary or visual material, ideas, suggestions of any nature whatsoever.

Therefore, as required, I am returning your correspondence unexamined and without retaining any copies.

We hope that you understand our policy. Good luck and thank you for your interest in Jerry Bruckheimer Films.

Sincerely,

Ally Hawkins
Development Associate

Enclosures

Zack Sternwalker
P.O. Box #22883
Oakland, CA 94609

Tom Cruise
c/o Kevin Huvane
Creative Artists Agency LLC (CAA-LA)
9830 Wilshire Blvd Beverly Hills, CA 90201

DEAR TOM CRUISE,

Let me begin by telling you that you are, hands down, my third favorite actor of all time.

Please don't be upset that I didn't rank you higher, however, as you have a quality that my first and second choices simply don't possess. I'm speaking of that unique ability to mold your persona for ANY role, which brings me to the point of this letter.

I couldn't help but notice your recent hiatus from the moviemaking business and I'd like to propose a new project that I've written with you in mind.

Allow me to recount the origin of my idea.

I've recently become unemployed and have been lying around the house listening to my mother's old Sammy Davis

Jr. records. One day it occurred to me that no one had ever told Sammy's story through the medium of film.

Immediately I began a screenplay, and two days later I'd pared down my draft to a tight thousand pages.

Allow me to give you a brief plot treatment.

Our story takes place in China just around the turn of the century and focuses on the last week of Sammy's life when, in a bizarre bathing accident, his right foot is tragically severed. Putting his faith in science, he undergoes a risky procedure where the foot of a dead panda is surgically attached to his leg. He must then learn to live with his deformity and still find time to practice for the all-China song and dance competition only a few days away.

Working titles are: *Little Dancing Panda*, *Watch Him Sing Softly*, *The Story of Sammy Davis Sr.'s Son*, and *Candy Corn Cadillac*.

Now I know what you're thinking: "How could I, Tom Cruise, ever play Sammy Davis Jr.?" Don't worry because I did some research and found a couple really good books on how to dance and sing just like Sammy did. I can even move some furniture around my room and as long as we're really quiet after my mom goes to bed (10 pm) we can practice in there.

Please don't be skeptical of my experiences in the filmmaking business either. This is my second screenplay and I'm currently working with Jerry Bruckheimer on the first.

If you're available sometime this week I'd like to come by your house and get your foot size so I can find some appropriate dance shoes (I might have to get them at a secondhand store as I am a bit low on cash). Please contact me with your schedule of availability.

I hope to hear from you soon.

ZACK STERNWALKER

P.S. As a sign of good faith, please accept this complimentary vampire.

CREATIVE ARTISTS AGENCY

LITERARY AND TALENT AGENCY

9830 WILSHIRE BOULEVARD
BEVERLY HILLS, CALIFORNIA 90212-1825
TELEPHONE: 310-288-4545 • FACSIMILE: 310-288-4800

November 8

Mr. Zack Sternwalker
P.O. Box 22883
Oakland, CA 94609

RE: ZACK STERNWALKER - AGENCY REPRESENTATION - WORKING TITLES:
"LITTLE DANCING PANDA," "WATCH HIM SING SOFTLY," "THE STORY
OF SAMMIE DAVIS SR.'S SON" AND "CANDY CORN CADILLAC"

Dear Mr. Sternwalker:

We received your letter dated October 5, 2004 requesting to submit literary material to
Creative Artists Agency for Tom Cruise. Although we appreciate your interest, we have
a firm policy of returning all unsolicited material unread. Accordingly, we enclose the
letter that you submitted.

Your unsolicited submission has not been, and will not be disclosed to any executive or
other employee of Creative Artists Agency or any other person. You should be aware that
many ideas are generated by our employees and our clients or other sources. To the
extent that any projects are generated which contain elements similar to what you
submitted, the similarities are purely coincidental.

Thank you for considering Mr. Cruise. We wish you much luck in your endeavors.

Cordially,

CREATIVE ARTISTS AGENCY

Submissions Dept.

Submissions Department

Enclosure

cc: Kevin Huvane

Zack Sternwalker
P.O. Box #22883
Oakland, CA 94609

Wild Birds Unlimited
Franchise Support Center
11711 N. College. Ave.
Suite #146
Carmel, IN 46032

DEAR WILD BIRDS UNLIMITED,

I'd like to begin by congratulating you on your large selection of bird feeders. It's a pleasure to know that some companies still care about showing people the beauty of nature located right in their own backyard.

Recently I've become unemployed and have been forced to move back in with my mother. To occupy my time I've been writing screenplays for various top Hollywood players (I expect you'll be seeing some of the films out in theaters next summer). Unfortunately, all this writing has caused me to seriously stress out.

In an effort to help me relax during my writing breaks, my mother recently purchased one of your fine bird feeders. Since then I've spend many afternoons sitting outside on the back porch, drinking lemonade and watching little birds flutter about, which brings me to the point of this letter.

For some strange reason your feeder only attracts very small, boring birds like the house sparrow. It's not that I don't like to observe these small birds, it's just that I'd like to see the occasional larger bird, like a hawk or pelican. It would be so wonderful to one day come outside and see a majestic bald eagle swoop down to my bird feeder for its morning meal.

Eager to understand the problem, I did some research and discovered that amazingly, these larger birds don't even eat the birdseed that you've provided! On the contrary, most of them subsist on a meat-based diet, be it fish, snakes, rodents, or even other smaller birds.

Now I don't want to sit here and just complain about the flaws in your product—I'd rather help improve them.

I think the basic idea of a feeder that hangs from the porch is a good one. However, what would happen if we took away the birdseed and replaced it with an assortment of dead animals?

From what I've read about the habits of these larger birds, it wouldn't be long before they spotted the little corpses and arrived, salivating from the beak (have you ever seen an eagle salivate? Me neither. That's why I'm so excited for this project).

So what would be my role? Well, I happen to know of a very well-priced seafood restaurant nearby. I'm sure they'd sell us a good variety of fish at a very low price. Also I can set up traps around the neighborhood to catch various rats and squirrels that could serve as food for the birds.

Ironically, I've found that your current feeders happen to be a great resource for catching small birds as well as observing them. All I have to do is aim my BB gun and fire. Even though I'm a terrible shot, I almost always kill something.

If everything goes according to plan, I'm confident I can accumulate enough food after a month to fill up about ten feeders. I'm even open to those fancy scientific techniques like freeze-drying, where the dead animals are preserved for shipping.

Because I'm just heading up this project, it seems fair that I also get a creative voice in the commercial spots.

Allow me to give you a brief treatment of my best idea.

The scene opens on a baby as it crawls out into a backyard. It looks around and smiles, possibly hiccupping.

All of a sudden we hear the blood-curdling screech of an eagle and watch in wonder as it swoops down and clamps its talons into the head of the child, lifting it from the ground.

Working names for the new feeder are: *Raptor Watch 9000*, *The Big Bird Eater*, or *Just a Beak of Nature*.

I'd like to invite your representatives by for some lemonade and a quick demo of how I envision the new feeder working (the early morning or dusk hours would probably be best). Please contact me immediately with a convenient date.

Hope to hear from you soon.

ZACK STERNWALKER

P.S. As a sign of good faith, please accept this complimentary vampire.

Zack Sternwalker
P.O. Box #22883
Oakland, CA 94609

Paul McCartney
c/o Staff member
Paul Freundlich Associates Media
451 Greenwich St. #503
New York, NY 10013

DEAR PAUL MCCARTNEY,

Let me begin by saying how much I love your old band, The Beatles. I do not believe the songs are racist propaganda aimed at the Chinese as many of the music "critics" have argued over the years.

In fact, I've collected both albums and spent many nights selecting my favorite tracks and playing them for my less musically educated friends—which brings me to the point of this letter.

Wouldn't it be great if the everyday music fan, who may not have the patience to collect both Beatles albums (not all of us know where those obscure record stores are) could still enjoy the best songs on a nifty little compilation record?

I know artists don't like to look at their body of work as having bests, but let's be honest for a moment. There is no way you can compare the boring chirp of "Peaceful Easy Feeling" with the masterful storytelling of "Hotel California." It's obvious you and John Lennon went to very dark corners of your mind to compose the latter and I wouldn't want the listener jolted from those vividly painted scenes.

Here is where my expertise comes in.

Not only do I know all the Beatles songs (and yes I've heard that all-Hebrew version of "Desperado" that you guys did at the '74 Israeli Freedom Concert) but I also have the rare ability to tap into the likes and dislikes of the common listener. Also, I've recently become unemployed so I can now devote all my time to the project.

My role would be to select the tracks, burn them onto one CD, then add a little oboe where it feels appropriate (trust me on this one).

Working titles for the compilation are: *It's Finally Time for The Beatles*, *Just he Best of The Beatles*, *Hotel California and Other Really Good The Beatles Songs*, and *The Beatles Are Back Forever*.

As I stated earlier, I can be responsible for organizing the tracks, adding some extras, and then burning a final copy.

However, I can't afford to do a lot of them because blank CDs are too expensive for my current budget.

Instead, why don't you swing by my place sometime next week so we can drive over to *CompUSA* (it's five minutes from my house) and get a few of those bulk packs on your credit card. And don't worry, the few bucks you spend now will be reimbursed to you when the final product hits the music stores.

Please let me know when you'll be coming by, and if you have any suggestions for the cover art (I was thinking of a scene depicting you and the other members spearing a wild boar).

Hope to hear from you soon.

ZACK STERNWALKER

P.S. As a sign of good faith, please accept these complimentary vampires.

Zack Sternwalker
P.O. Box #22883
Oakland, CA 94609

Kraft Foods Global, Inc
Three Lakes Drive
Northfield, IL 68093

DEAR KRAFT,

I'd like to first thank you for making such wonderful food products. Seems like every time I turn around your company has introduced another item to the grocery store aisle.

Although I'm aware of your many products and quite convinced of their quality, I'm embarrassed to say I've only recently tried my first one. I'm speaking, of course, about your delicious macaroni and cheese.

And what an easy dish to prepare! When I first looked in the box and saw all that pasta I wondered if I'd gotten in over my head. But with a little help from my mother (I recently moved back home after my wife left me and I lost my job) I was able to boil it and then add the proper amounts of milk and butter. In no time at all I was able to prepare the dish entirely on my own—which I did nearly every day.

Despite this wonderful development in my life, I also began to notice that I was putting on a great deal of weight.

Concerned about my health, I did some research and found out that the cheese packet you include is very high in fat and cholesterol. This, combined with all that butter and milk, make for a very fattening meal.

But please don't get me wrong. I love your macaroni and cheese and I still plan on eating it every day for the rest of my life. I'd just like to make a small improvement so it also caters to those of us keeping an eye on their waistline.

Allow me to explain the origins of my idea.

Curious about the wild world of nutrition (and my place in that world), I set out for my local library. After reading all the important medical books, I learned that most doctors recommend eating a balanced diet consisting mostly of fruits, vegetables, grains, and proteins—not just macaroni and cheese.

Now I think we both know that no one ever really follows these guidelines exactly. But it is safe to say that people try to incorporate one or two of these healthier items into their diet. This is why I recommend that you introduce a new dish, which I've cleverly named *Kraft Macaroni and Cheese and Carrots*, to your extensive product line.

As you can probably guess I simply made a slight addition to the original recipe. Now when someone eats a plate of your macaroni and cheese they also get the full nutritional value found in one medium-sized carrot.

So how did I do it? Well, first I went to the store and picked out one box of your premium macaroni and cheese. But instead of immediately going to the checkout stand like I'd done previously, I walked over to the produce section and picked out a nice-looking carrot (if it's orange it's probably ripe). Later on, I cut the carrot into little pieces and threw it in with the pasta. This way I could boil both the pasta and carrot at the same time.

And please don't be skeptical at my selection of the carrot as the featured vegetable. Not only is it highly nutritional (they say it helps your vision), it also reminds people of how much they love rabbits—which I took into account when thinking of a new advertising campaign.

Now obviously we can't use a real rabbit to endorse this product because they don't speak clearly enough. But we could dress someone up to look like a rabbit. In fact, on a recent visit to the costume shop I happened upon a very flattering rabbit outfit in my exact size.

I propose that we do a couple of commercial spots featuring myself as the rabbit.

To grab people's attention I will dash in and out of rush-hour traffic while eating a plate of our *Kraft Macaroni and Cheese and Carrots*. When people see how agile the rabbit is they'll immediately want to eat exactly what it eats. That's when we flash the product name across the bottom of the screen.

And please don't be concerned that my current weight problem might hinder my ability to dodge speeding cars. I'm still very quick on my feet and as long as I do some light stretching beforehand, I should have no problems.

If at all possible I would like for your representatives to come by sometime next week and watch me do a few sprints up and down the block wearing the rabbit suit. Please contact me with your schedule of availability.

I hope to hear from you soon.   ZACK STERNWALKER

P.S. As a sign of good faith, please accept this complimentary vampire.

Zack Sternwalker
P.O. Box #22883
Oakland, CA 94609

Hulk Hogan
130 Willadel Dr.
Belleair, FL 33756

DEAR HULK HOGAN,

Let me be the first to congratulate you on your spectacular wrestling career. From what I remember you were good at throwing your opponent down on the mat.

This being said, I haven't really seen much of you lately. And please don't think I'm not looking. Every night after I get done cutting the pant legs off my Levi's jeans I settle down in front of the television to watch the WWF wrestling program. I put on my Hulk Hogan t-shirt. I put on my Hulk Hogan headband. But where is Hulk Hogan?

I've written several long letters to the local television station demanding an explanation as to why they never let you wrestle but I've yet to get a reply (don't you hate it when people avoid things?).

Anyway, I'm not writing this letter just to complain. On the contrary, I'd like to propose a project that will thrust you back into the limelight.

Please allow me to explain.

The other day I was sitting around the house listening to my mom's old Sammy Davis, Jr. records (I've been out of work since my wife left me and I was forced to move back in with my mother) when I glanced over at the morning paper. According to the news we're supposed to be recognizing Christopher Columbus Day. At first I passed off this notice purely because it was the news (isn't it all so boring?). But after a while I began to wonder who this Christopher Columbus guy was.

With curiosity eating heartily at my brain, I set out for my local library. I did some intense research and discovered that Christopher Columbus was actually this famous sailor who discovered America. Apparently he spent the better part of his life torturing and killing the Indians who were living here.

I was so excited by this story that I went home and took out my typewriter, determined to write a brilliant screenplay that would bring the Christopher Columbus story to the screen.

Strangely, I hit an immediate writer's block. So in order to relax and let the "idea machine" (that's what I call my brain) get cooking, I went out back and shot small birds with my BB gun. Just as I was in the middle of putting a house sparrow out of its misery, the idea hit me: Why not combine my favorite wrestler with my newest screenplay? Thus, the Christopher Columbus screenplay began to flow out of me like hot, burning urine.

Please allow me to give you a brief plot treatment.

Our story begins the day your ship arrives in the new world. Exhausted from being out at sea, you triumphantly run ashore and rub the sand on your face, tasting it and feeling its coolness (this scene should be acted very sensuously so that the everyday viewer can feel your emotion to the fullest extent).

Slowly you look up and see several Indians approaching. They are smiling and carrying gifts.

Then, just as they get close enough, you charge them and piledrive one man into the sand. As his friend tries to help, you expertly clothesline him and apply one of your trademark Hulk Hogan holds.

The film takes many twists and turns after that—too many for me to explain at this time. I will tell you that the climactic scene takes place in a giant metal cage and involves you wrestling fifty naked Indians, one of whom you've developed a serious love interest with.

Some working titles are: *Cross My Heart and Hope To Die*, *Against the Ropes: The Story of Christopher Columbus Day*, and *How to Peel a Spanish Banana*.

I was also thinking that you could talk to some of your wrestling friends about playing some of the minor roles, but that's something we can discuss further down the line.

If all goes well I think I can secure Francis Ford Coppola as the director (he was the genius behind the film *Sleepless in Seattle*).

Please contact me immediately with your decision on whether you'd like to be involved in this project. I hope to hear from you soon.

ZACK STERNWALKER

P.S. As a sign of good faith, please accept this complimentary vampire.

Zack Sternwalker
P.O. Box #22883
Oakland, CA 94609

Dunkin' Donuts Consumer Care
14 Placella Park Drive
Randolph, MA 02368

DEAR DUNKIN' DONUTS,

Let me begin by congratulating you on your wonderful donut shop. Every once in a while, if I feel I've earned it, I treat myself to one of your delicious glazed donuts alongside my mornsing coffee.

In fact, I'd like to eat your donuts a lot more (I love to support a good local business) but I have to stay away because of a recent weight problem brought on by my traumatic divorce.

Currently, I begin my day with a hot cup of coffee and a piece of toast which I prepare myself. While this is fine for now, I find it boring eating my toast and coffee alone in my house (actually it's my mom's house but she says I can have it when she dies).

The thing is, I'd really like to eat my breakfast in a more social environment with other people who are also starting out their day. Since I can't eat donuts on a regular basis, I wonder if you would be open to the idea of adding toast to your menu?

I did notice that you incorporated bagels in the past couple of years and I think this is a step in the right direction. If you start selling toast I'm confident that other people who are challenged by an ever-increasing waistline will take great solace in the fact that they can still frequent your shop without betraying their diets.

And I know what you may be thinking: is toast really that much more healthy than donuts?

Actually it is. In fact, I've been doing a bit of research lately and have read that doctors recommend a daily intake of grains as an essential part of a healthy diet. Toast is made up of these necessary grains while donuts are just fried dough that has been glazed with a heavy coat of sugar.

Now, I realize I may have come on a little strong barking out suggestions about where and when to sell toast. But don't worry, I'm willing to help. In a stroke of good luck I've recently become unemployed. I also know how to make a great piece of toast (a lot of people think they're doing it right, but they're not).

In addition to my toasting abilities, I'm also very familiar with all the popular spreads including: butter, margarine, jam, and even ketchup (it sounds unappetizing but I met a guy from Nebraska who swore that it added an extra two inches to his erection).

Here is my proposal.

If you could give me a portion of your counter space I can take over all the toast-making responsibilities. I have a fairly good toaster that I'm sure my mom would loan us until we made the money to buy our own. Then, if you could front the cost of the various spreads, we'd be well on our way.

At this point, I can commit to working the toast counter at least two hours a day (that should sufficiently cover the breakfast period) and then put in a good half hour for the necessary clean up, i.e., putting the used breads back in their respective bags, capping the spreads, and washing the butter knives.

In addition to the preparation I'd also like to help with the advertising.

Instead of a commercial, I propose that we build a gigantic piece of toast and perch it atop your shop. Then, and only if you feel up to it, we can add a small square of butter (this would also be constructed out of cement and painted a bright yellow). This image will let the public know that Dunkin' Donuts is now very serious about toast (serious about loving it, that is).

I would like for your representatives to come by my house sometime next week and see me in action (I wouldn't want you to hire without seeing my abilities).

Please let me know your schedule of availability as well as the type of spread your representatives like (my mom is going grocery shopping tomorrow and could probably pick some up for the demo).

I hope to hear from you soon.

ZACK STERNWALKER

P.S. As a sign of good faith, please accept this complimentary vampire.

Zack Sternwalker
P.O. Box #22883
Oakland, CA 94609

General Electric Appliance Headquarters
AP6 Room #129
Louisville, KY 40225

DEAR GENERAL ELECTRIC,

Let me first congratulate you on establishing such a good reputation in the field of home appliances.

Although you probably have an extensive team of inventors at your disposal, I've recently come up with a new product that I would like to run by you.

Allow me to recount my story of its discovery.

A few months ago I fell upon some hard times and was forced to move back in with my mother. This emotionally difficult time, coupled with her fully stocked refrigerator, caused me to put on a great deal of weight.

After staring too many times down the cold barrel of my bathroom scale, I decided to turn my life around. I put myself on a strict diet (plenty of carrots) and woke up every morning for a brisk one-mile walk.

As you may have guessed, this high-intensity exercise often left me sweating and out of breath, desperate for a cold glass of juice. So, on one such morning, I walked straight over to our recently purchased General Electric brand refrigerator.

While I originally intended to simply open the door and get some juice, the sudden blast of cool air refreshed me to such an extent that I no longer needed the juice at all. Instead, I felt so revived I set out on another walk—this time two blocks longer. Pretty soon I was up to two or three morning walks, taking a five minute break between to crawl inside the refrigerator (I removed some of the condiment shelves) and cool off.

This brings me to the point of this letter: Would it be possible to build a refrigerator exclusively for humans?

Think of how convenient it would be for active people to simply take a break and step inside their *Refrigerator for Humans* (as I've coined it) only to emerge seconds later completely refreshed and ready for more exercise.

The *Refrigerator for Humans* could also come in a variety of sizes. Luckily, I happen to know a great deal of people who vary in size and who will serve well as test models. For example, my neighbor Neil is quite tall and slender (he likes to play tennis). On the other hand my mailman, Clark, is short and a bit overweight (he's an alcoholic). Using the people around me, I could establish three or four general sizes (small, medium, large, bigger) and submit the designs for each *Refrigerator for Humans* to your company.

Then, when it comes time to introduce this product to the public I could devise a clever commercial to capture the public's attention.

Allow me to share my current idea.

Since the *Refrigerator for Humans* is a product aimed at active people, the commercial should be one of action. I envision the acclaimed actor, Charles Bronson, engaged in a violent fistfight with a pregnant woman.

The camera moves in and we see him bloody, obviously losing the match . . . that is until he takes a moment to hop inside his *Refrigerator for Humans*.

Seconds later he emerges, the blood gone from his face and his muscles rejuvenated. Subsequently, he beats the woman to the ground, then reaches into her chest and pulls out her beating heart. He places the heart in his pocket, then gets in his car and drives to the nearby hospital.

Once inside, he gives the heart to the first doctor he sees, then makes a "thumbs-up" gesture towards the camera.

This ad will alert the viewer that the *Refrigerator for Humans* is new on the scene and that it's ready to get things done.

Please contact me with any relevant suggestions and list some possible times your representatives can come by my house and view the design sketches.

Hope to hear from you soon.

ZACK STERNWALKER

P.S. As a sign of good faith, please accept this complimentary vampire.

Zack Sternwalker
P.O. Box #22883
Oakland, CA 94609

Taco Bell Consumer Affairs
17901 Von Karman
Irving, CA 92614-6221

DEAR TACO BELL,

Let me begin by congratulating you on your excellent restaurant chain.

Ever since I was a little boy I've loved Mexican food. Unfortunately, I rarely ate it because of the tremendous preparation time required for most of the dishes.

This is why I like what you've done. Now when I want Mexican food I can go to your establishment and know that I'll be eating my burrito in less than five minutes after ordering it. This allows me to spend less of my life waiting for Mexican food and more of it doing productive things, like shooting small birds with my BB gun.

Despite how pleased I am with your restaurant chain, I have noticed something that could use some improvement.

I'm speaking, of course, about your current advertising campaign.

I can see why you emphasize your healthy menu and use of fresh ingredients, but to be completely honest it's a little boring. Instead, why not try something a little more personal.

As you may have guessed, I'm hinting towards the introduction of a new Taco Bell mascot.

Throughout history corporate mascots have used humor and joy to introduce would-be customers to various products that could improve their lives. And besides that, they're just plain fun!

To come up with an appropriate mascot for your restaurant I used myself as the target of some intense consumer research. After observing my habits closely, I discovered I was most inclined to visit your establishment when I was extremely happy (when I'm depressed I just lie around the house listening to old Sammy Davis Jr. records).

So what is the all-time greatest character used to make people happy? The clown. So, without further ado I'd like to introduce you to Taco Bell's new mascot: *The Taco Clown*.

Please allow me to bring you up to speed on this wonderful character.

At first glance *The Taco Clown* appears as a normal clown—i.e., funny nose, makeup, pie in the face, etc. However on closer inspection we discover that he is a clown who only eats tacos. And what's more—he only eats Taco Bell tacos. Thus, if someone were to walk up to *The Taco Clown* and offer him a hamburger, he'd surely refuse it.

Incorporating a clown into the fast food industry is a good idea—not only because clowns are hysterical, but also because it's never been done before.

Now you may be asking—where do I fit in? Well, I've recently become unemployed and been forced to move back in with my mother. While this has left me somewhat depressed, it's also given me plenty of free time to come up with great ideas like this one.

Here is my proposal.

I did some research and discovered there are actual businesses near my residence that make their own money by renting out costumes. Even better, they offer a wide selection of clown outfits.

Since *The Taco Clown* is my creation I think it best that I be the actor selected for the part. While I have limited acting experience (I have talked my way out of a few speeding tickets) I am blessed with that rare positivity required to make people smile. Also I have many wonderful commercial ideas up my sleeve.

Please allow me to give a brief plot treatment of my favorite.

The camera opens on a restaurant scene at one of the many, low-quality, fast food hamburger establishments. People are eating quietly, occasionally sipping a beverage.

All of a sudden *The Taco Clown* jumps through the window of the restaurant, sending shattered glass everywhere. He then takes out a semi-automatic weapon and fires a few warning shots into the ceiling. After getting everyone's attention, *The Taco Clown* announces that he has compiled detailed personal information on each person in the restaurant.

He then issues an ultimatum, that if they don't pledge to only eat at Taco Bell for the rest of their lives, he'll hunt down and kill every one of them.

But I don't want to undertake this project alone. Instead I propose that you send some of your representatives by my house sometime in the next couple of weeks (preferably in the afternoon because I like to sleep in) and we'll drive over to the costume shop and take a look at the various clown costumes they have to choose from.

Please write back with any relevant suggestions and let me know the days and times that fit best with your schedule. I hope to hear from you soon.

ZACK STERNWALKER

P.S. As a sign of good faith, please accept this complimentary vampire.

Taco Bell Corp.
17901 Von Karman
Irvine, CA 92614
Tel 949-863-4500
Fax 949-863-3801

November 9

Zack Sternwalker
P.O. Box 22883
Oakland, CA 94609

Dear Mr. Sternwalker:

On behalf of Taco Bell Corp. ("Taco Bell"), I want to thank you for your interest in our Company and for taking the time and effort to suggest an idea.

We have, however, adopted a general policy of not accepting unsolicited ideas and suggestions. While we regularly receive many unsolicited suggestions concerning our advertising, products, processes, and a wide range of other subjects, experience has shown that most of the unsolicited ideas we receive have already been considered or used by Taco Bell or its competitors. Also, experience has proven that the practice of considering unsolicited suggestions can give rise to misunderstandings as to the origin and ownership of the particular ideas which may be contained in such materials.

In keeping with this policy, we are unable to pursue unsolicited suggestions; and have not retained any copies of your letter. May I express our appreciation for your interest in our company and sincerely thank you for taking time to write, by enclosing a "Taco Bell Gift Check" for your use.

Very truly yours,

Legal Department

Zack Sternwalker
P.O. Box #22883
Oakland, CA 94609

Levi Strauss & Co.
1155 Battery Street
San Francisco, CA 94111

DEAR LEVI STRAUSS,

Let me begin by saying how much I love your product. Ever since I was little, I've worn your pants both for protection and warmth. In addition to their functionality I also like how you've taken the time to introduce many new colors and styles (baggy, straight leg, stone-washed, etc.). This being said, I've noticed a large problem that should be brought to your attention.

Please allow me to explain.

Recently, I put on a great deal of weight due to my long and painful divorce. In an effort to get back into shape, I changed my diet and began a rigorous morning walk.

It was during this heavy physical activity that I noticed a strange occurrence. For the first time in my life your pants kept my legs too warm.

When I'd finished my morning walk and was preparing to step into my refrigerator to cool off (it actually works really well), I noticed a heavy coat of perspiration on my inner thighs.

As with many things in life, what often begins as a minor nuisance can quickly escalate into a serious problem. Pretty soon all that heat and sweat on my legs caused me to develop a terrible rash. I went to the doctor (actually he's not really a doctor but he did take a few CPR classes in college) and he suggested I buy a special rash cream from the drugstore.

Taking his advice to heart, I took a brisk walk over to my local Walgreen's (it's a new store that sells over-the-counter drugs as well as various other household items).

To my horror the special rash cream my doctor had prescribed was being sold for the outrageous price of $8.99! To make a long story short, I realized I wasn't going to be able to afford this medical luxury and I would have to use my own creativity to solve the problem.

After many days spent deep in thought, I finally came up with an interesting idea.

I borrowed my mom's scissors (oh yeah, I live with my mom now) and took out one of my favorite pairs of Levi's. I realized that my legs were probably getting so sweaty and hot because they weren't receiving enough outside air to cool them off. Therefore, I decided to cut off a substantial portion of the pant legs (don't worry, I only did it to one pair).

What resulted was the same Levi's pants—except now about 2/3 of the fabric covering my lower legs was gone (my mom said she would use the leftover fabric for rags).

Putting my hypothesis into practice I wore my new cut-off Levi's pants the very next morning. When I returned home and took off my clothes I was overjoyed to discover the skin on my inner thigh was smooth and cool to the touch. Since then I've worn my new pair of Levi's *Shorters*—which I've cleverly named—every time I exert myself physically.

Now, as I sit here writing this letter, I'm pleased to announce that I've returned to my original weight, my rash has disappeared, and as of late I've even been enjoying some casual glances from the opposite sex!

Since my invention of the Levi's *Shorters* has changed my life so much it would make me so happy to bring my discovery to others who may also be suffering from a similar situation.

Here is my proposal.

Your company can send me a whole bunch of pairs of Levi's pants and I then I can do the necessary cutting (I guess my mom will have plenty of rags now!). Once they're finished, I can send the new pairs of Levi's *Shorters* back to your company and you can ship them out to the retail stores of your choosing.

Now, I realize that not all products are a success right off the bat. This is why I'm also willing to help create the unique ad campaign.

Since this product is so great at keeping legs cool, there should be plenty of close-up shots at calf level. As much as I'd like to use my own legs (I want to be a star too), I also know people don't like to see a lot of unsightly hair.

This is why I've selected a very attractive celebrity spokesperson who has a great set of legs. I'm speaking of course about Christian Slater—the star of many of our most beloved American films (pay attention and you'll see his brief cameo as the hot dog vender in *Sleepless in Seattle*).

Now I know you're wondering how we'd work around the obvious fact that Christian is a male and probably has hair on his legs just like me. Well, I happen to be working on a very interesting film with him in the upcoming months in which he'll be put on a strict regimen of female hormones. If all goes well, his legs will be smooth and silky by the beginning of production.

I'd like your company to contact me with a schedule of when your representatives are available to come by my house and see me model a pair of the *Shorters*. Hope to hear from you soon.

ZACK STERNWALKER

P.S. As a sign of good faith, please accept this complimentary vampire.

Zack Sternwalker
P.O. Box #22883
Oakland, CA 94609

Tupperware Corporation
Attn: Customer Care
P.O. Box #2353
Orlando, FL 32802

DEAR TUPPERWARE,

I'd like to begin by congratulating you on your wonderful line of Tupperware products. Finally people are able to stop worrying about how their food is stored and focus on more important things in their lives.

For example, I cook a large portion of *Kraft Macaroni and Cheese and Carrots* every night. Sometimes I just can't finish it all (I have to listen when my body says it's full). Thanks to your Tupperware I can now eat the leftovers for lunch even if I have to spend the entire day at the costume shop trying on various rabbit outfits. This being said, I've noticed one small area for improvement.

Please allow me to explain. Recently I've been getting very interested in nutrition. In my studies I've noticed that most doctors recommend eating a piece of fruit every day.

Now I'll be honest with you. I don't like apples. And I don't like oranges either. But after consulting the produce manager at my local supermarket he recommended I give pears a try. After eating just one, I liked it so much that I returned and bought a dozen more (sometimes all you have to do is ask!).

That night when I was preparing my bag lunch for the following day, I threw in a pear along with my container of *Kraft Macaroni and Cheese and Carrots*.

Imagine my horror when I took out my lunch the following day only to find my pear had been mashed beyond all recognition. At first I thought it was just due to my extremely active lifestyle (sometimes my backpack bobs up and down when I walk too fast), but when I walked slower the following day, the results were still the same. Confused and depressed, I spent several days lying around the house listening to Sammy Davis, Jr. records. Then, inspired by his wonderful singing, I decided to tackle the pear problem using my own creativity (thanks again, Sammy).

Once my mom had gone to bed (I live with my mom since my wife left me and I lost my job) I melted down one of your Tupperware containers and molded the hot plastic into the shape of a pear. Then I put the container in the freezer to solidify.

In the morning I was pleased to find I had created the first ever *Tupperpear*.

I placed my pear inside it and then tossed it in my lunch bag. Later on at lunchtime I nervously reached inside my bag and pulled out my *Tupperpear*. I carefully opened the plastic container and to my joy saw that my pear was perfectly intact.

I ate my pear that day with a huge smile on my face. In fact, every day since has been filled with smiles.

Now I know I'm not unique. I'm sure many people are suffering from this same dilemma. This is why I'd like to work with your company to introduce the *Tupperpear* to the general public.

Here is my proposal.

Since I can't keep melting down plastic containers in my home (my mom says it stinks up the house too much) I propose that you take the production responsibilities off my shoulders. This will leave me ample free time to work on the important ad campaign.

Please don't think that this is some way for me to pass off all the work to you. On the contrary, I've already written ten commercial scripts that are ready to be put into production.

Allow me to give you a brief treatment of the best.

We open with a man getting viciously beaten by a group of angry school children.

All of a sudden one child picks up a large rock and smashes it into the man's crotch. He screams so loudly that the children all step back. Then they watch in horror as he reaches into his pants and pulls a mashed pear from his underwear.

He looks into the camera and says, "I wish I had my *Tupperpear*". That's when we flash the product name across the screen.

It'd be great if your representatives could come by my house sometime in the next couple of weeks and take a look at my test model. Please contact me with your schedule of availability.

I hope to hear from you soon.   ZACK STERNWALKER

P.S. As a sign of good faith, please accept this complimentary vampire.

Zack Sternwalker
P.O. Box #22883
Oakland, CA 94609

Irish Spring
300 Park Avenue
New York, NY 10022

DEAR IRISH SPRING,

I'd like to first congratulate you on your product. Whenever I need to clean a part of my body I'm always confident that your soap will do the job.

Also, I like how after I bathe, I smell more or less like your bar of soap. It's almost like your soap is both a cleaning product as well as a perfume—have you thought of bottling the scent?

Anyway, I'm getting off subject. The real reason I've contacted your company is to propose a possible collaboration on a new product I've invented.

Please allow me to recount the story of my discovery.

The other day I was dining out at my favorite Mexican restaurant, Taco Bell. I was eating a Burrito Supreme and drinking a large Coca-Cola when all of a sudden I felt a great pain in my lower abdomen. I jumped up, ran to the counter and asked to be buzzed into the bathroom (they tend to keep the bathroom locked because sometimes non-customers try to use it).

Once inside, I sat down on the toilet and proceeded to have one of the largest bowel movements of my entire life. Afterwards I was so relaxed that in the process of wiping I made an awkward movement and accidentally got fecal matter on my hand.

Being a very health conscious person I quickly went to the bathroom sink and prepared to clean up. First I turned on the hot water. Then I pulled the lever on the mechanical soap dispenser (I'm sure you know what I'm talking about being that you're in the soap business).

Unfortunately, this particular soap dispenser did not dispense. I immediately yelled for assistance but for some reason no one came (I bet the employees couldn't hear me because of all the loud, bean-cooking machines).

Growing more concerned, I glanced around the sink and saw that someone had placed a small bar of soap near the faucet. My first instinct was to go ahead and pick it up but then I began to think: Where had this soap been? It was all slimy and looked as if it had been used by many people in my similar position.

In the end I decided to leave the bathroom without washing my hands. But since I was still hungry I went ahead and finished my meal, even pausing at one point to nibble up a chunk of refried bean that had fallen into the palm of my hand.

As you may have guessed, I awoke the next morning feeling quite ill (it really is true what they say about washing your hands after using the bathroom).

After spending a few days under the weather, I decided to take steps to prevent a possible reoccurrence of this situation. I went into my bathroom and grabbed my private bar of Irish Spring soap (actually my mom uses it too but it's okay because she's clean).

I took a piece of string and tied one end around the bar of soap. Then I tied the other end to the belt loop on my Levi's jeans. Although I looked a little strange with a bar of soap hanging off my pants, I was now fully equipped to wash my hands in any public restroom.

Because I'm not a selfish person, I would like your company to help me introduce this new product—which I've cleverly named *Soap on a String*—to the general public.

One of the great things about this product is that it can go anywhere, on anyone. For example, say you find yourself very dirty and in the middle of the Sahara desert. If you were wearing a *Soap on a String* all you'd have to do is go to the nearest public restroom and you'd be okay.

But I don't want to be that guy who just sits on the sidelines yelling out various inventions he thinks you should manufacture—I want to help.

On my end, I've contacted the local string store and secured several large spools. All you have to do is send me a whole bunch of soap and I'll do the necessary tying.

But before we jump ahead of ourselves I think it would be wise for you and your representatives to come by my house to see the original *Soap on a String* in action (I've got a good test sink). Please contact me with your schedule of availability.

I hope to hear from you soon.   ZACK STERNWALKER

P.S. As a sign of good faith, please accept this complimentary vampire.

COLGATE-PALMOLIVE COMPANY
A Delaware Corporation

300 Park Avenue
New York, NY 10022-7499
Household Products
800-338-8388
Personal Care Products
800-221-4607

Consumer Affairs Department

November 19

Mr Zack Sternwalker
Po Box 22883
Oakland CA 94609

Dear Mr Sternwalker:

Thank you for taking the time to contact us.

We are always pleased to know what consumers have to say about our products. We regularly receive complimentary comments from consumers and often they suggest product or package improvements or may even have ideas for new products. We welcome this opportunity to explain our policy concerning unsolicited ideas.

Since our company employs researchers in our Technology Centers devoted to developing new products and improving existing ones, we do not solicit outside suggestions and ideas. We will, however, consider ideas that are patented or are the subject of a patent application. This policy protects both you and the company. If you hold a patent or have an application pending on your idea, please let us know and we will send you the appropriate release forms.

If you would like to apply for a patent for your new idea, you may find the enclosed brochure from the U. S. Department of Commerce, Patent and Trademark Office helpful.

Once again, thank you for taking the time to contact us. We hope this information is helpful.

Sincerely,

Lisa Brown
Consumer Affairs Representative
Consumer Affairs

TLB/CAP

3176209A

Zack Sternwalker
P.O. Box #22883
Oakland, CA 94609

Five Peaks Technology
Portable Toilets
1790 Sun Dolphin Drive
Muskegon, MI 49444-1833

DEAR PORT-O-POTTY,

On a recent trip to the county fair I had the privilege of using one of your fine portable restrooms. I was glad it was there too because I had just eaten two large chili dogs and badly needed to relieve myself.

Now despite my overall positive experience with your portable restrooms, I couldn't help but notice one strong area of improvement.

I'm speaking, of course, about the addition of a vase of fresh flowers.

Please allow me to explain.

Throughout time, the presence of plant life has been a necessary element for a healthy mind-state (the famous movie director Francis Ford Coppola once dropped his pants at a formal dinner party and declared, "Take them for granted, take them for fools, but don't take away their pretty flowers.")

Aside from their chemical ability to produce oxygen (it's true, I looked it up on the internet) they are also quite pleasing to look at. All too often my trips to the bathroom end with heavy physical and mental exhaustion. I cannot stress the importance of having something pretty nearby to calm me down (I also take a series of deep breaths).

Now I know what you're thinking: how could we ever find the time to put a vase of fresh flowers in every one of our portable restrooms?

Well, this is where I come in.

Recently I've become unemployed and been forced to move back in with my mother. While this has been somewhat of a difficult step for me, it has been a good motivator for getting my life back on track (I'm convinced that if I take one step a day, for the rest of my life, I should have no trouble getting somewhere).

Since I have so much free time on my hands I propose that you employ me as the new *Port-O-Boy*, and give me the job of putting fresh flowers in every one of your portable restroom facilities each day. I've even designed a unique outfit made entirely from the toilet seat guards you provide (okay, it's true, I look at bit like a mummy, but as long as people see that I'm carrying flowers I don't think they'll be scared).

Also, I've recently met a girl (she looks a lot like Meg Ryan) who works at a flower shop. I don't usually mix business with pleasure, but since this is such a wonderful opportunity, I'm prepared to ask if her shop could work out a special rate for your company.

It would also be a good idea to get a head start on an advertising campaign. I envision a series of photos that depict the *Port-O-Boy* emerging valiantly from the rear ends of various farm animals (we could plaster these up around town).

I'd like to invite your representatives by my house sometime this week to discuss this project further. Please contact me with your schedule of availability (if it makes you feel more comfortable we can even have the business meeting in my mom's bathroom).

Hope to hear from you soon.   ZACK STERNWALKER

P.S. As a sign of good faith, please accept this complimentary vampire.

Zack Sternwalker
P.O. Box #22883
Oakland, CA 94609

Merriam-Webster, Inc.
47 Federal Street
P.O. Box #281
Springfield, MA 01102

DEAR MERRIAM-WEBSTER DICTIONARY,

Let me first congratulate you on assembling such an extensive collection of words.

I've spent many nights flipping through the pages and wondering how you could have completed such a detailed project. I'm a writer, so I can appreciate the difficulty of assembling words in a manner that keeps the reader's interest while at the same time providing necessary information.

This brings me to the point of this letter: Could it be possible that your book is *too* extensive?

Very often I don't have the time to sit down and thumb through your book, admiring its length. Instead I really need it to find a word. Now don't worry—although I've identified a crucial flaw in your material, I've also devised a solution.

Upon close examination of your book, I see that you have listed many obscure words along with their definitions. I think this is a wonderful idea as the general public probably doesn't know what these words mean.

However, I also see that you've included the definitions of many familiar words such as dog, cat, fun, pie, car, etc. I have nothing against these words and have in fact used them many times in personal conversation. However, in the interest of brevity, what would happen if we eliminated these types of words from your book altogether?

I think it would make the task of finding a more obscure word much easier. It's true, your dictionary would probably lose a bit of its impressiveness, but at the same time it would gain much more functionality.

Now I'm sure you're curious as to how I'd involve myself in this project (you didn't think I was just going to complain without offering any help, did you?).

In a stroke of bad luck, I've recently become unemployed and been forced to move back in with my mother. While this has been a very difficult emotional transition for me, it does give me ample free time to help.

Here is my proposal.

As it is my idea, I will act as chief editor in selecting the words. All you have to do is send me your newly printed dictionaries and I can go through each one and white out the unnecessary words.

If I work an eight-hour day, by my estimate I'll be able to edit 1.5 dictionaries per hour. I will then mail the books back to you for their normal shipment to retail stores. And since I'm going to use a lot of white-out it would also be helpful if you sent along a lasting supply.

Working titles for our new dictionary are: *Words That Really Matter*, *The Very Best of The Dictionary*, and *Sputum: A Merriam-Webster Reader.*.

Since this product may initially confuse many consumers I propose that we also hire a celebrity spokesperson to endorse it. This job requires someone who has a high level of intellectual enthusiasm consistent with our dictionary, which is why I propose Hulk Hogan (he was formerly a professional wrestler and has made many television appearances). I envision him tearing apart other, less superior dictionaries as he sits atop a small donkey.

Luckily, I will be working with him on an upcoming film and I'm quite confident he will accept this project as a personal favor to me.

Please write back with any relevant suggestions as well as some possible dates when we can meet to discuss the project further. Hope to hear from you soon.

ZACK STERNWALKER

P.S. As a sign of good faith, please accept this complimentary vampire.

Zack Sternwalker
P.O. Box #22883
Oakland, CA 94609

DEAR CHARLES BRONSON,

Let me begin by telling you that you are a fantastic actor. Although I recently rented your film *Death Wish*, simply because I wanted to see what a gun looked like, I found it difficult not to be sucked in by your complex character.

This being said, I am quite confused as to your recent absences from the moviemaking business (don't these Hollywood types know talent when it runs across the screen blowing people away?).

At first I thought I should write an aggressive letter (I don't write those kinds of letters very often) to my all-time favorite movie director, Francis Ford Coppola, demanding that he cast you in his current project, but then why should I ride his coattail? Instead, I took out my typewriter, made a tall glass of lemonade (one sip and I'm swept away to the magical Land of Acidic), and set right to work on my next screenplay.

Of course, I hit an immediate roadblock (hint: there is always a detour). I remember asking myself, "What would be the perfect role for you?" A science fiction epic? A historical drama: I had a momentary vision of you cast as Harriet Tubman in a low-budget remake of the classic film *Freedom Tunnel.*

After much debate, I decided to take a break and let my brain rest. I went outside to watch my bird feeder and brought along a book my mom had recommended to me (I guess I forgot to mention that I live with my mom since my wife left me and I lost my job).

The book is entitled *The Boy Who Wanted A Baby* and focuses on a young man who is obsessed with becoming pregnant and carrying his child to delivery. Although I was a little turned off by the bizarre title (people have such active imaginations), I decided to give it a try.

Boy am I glad that I did. The book was amazing and I read it in one sitting (actually I took a break to make another glass of lemonade—constant hydration is key). And maybe it was because I had been thinking of you earlier, but the whole time I was reading I envisioned you as the main character.

Now, I've never adapted a book into a screenplay before, but I thought, what better time than the present? Using my mom's highlighter (don't worry, I asked first), I marked some of the more important scenes and then set to work activating the story so it would be a complete visual experience (this is what I *do*).

Forty-five minutes later, I had completed a brilliant, two-hundred-page film script that would make any Hollywood bigwig wet their trousers.

Please allow me to give you a brief treatment.

The story begins just as you wake from a very moving dream. In it, you see yourself naked, nine months pregnant and flying through the sky in the middle of a violent snow storm. This stirring image fresh in your mind, you become determined to get pregnant at all costs.

After breakfast, you visit your neighbor—who is also a powerful wizard (he wears a wizard hat, so don't worry about people not finding this believable). You tell him that you are willing to do *anything* if he will only cast a spell that will impregnate you. When he hears this, he immediately goes into a little dance (you don't know this at the time, but this is his special "warm-up dance" that he always does before casting a spell).

He then takes you out into his backyard and shows you this gigantic pile of human feces, which he commands you to eat. You're a bit hesitant at first, but then you remember your dream and how wonderful it felt to be pregnant. You slowly walk over and begin eating, only to discover that it tastes just like strawberry jam.

You finish it in no time and turn around to face the wizard, eagerly awaiting your prize. He nods and then begins another dance, this time way more complex. He gets faster and faster, and as he does, you feel your belly begin to grow. Soon the wizard is dancing so fast he's just a little ball of light, bouncing through the air. You look down and see that your stomach is now gigantic.

All of a sudden the wizard falls to the ground, completely exhausted. You run over, and as you're helping him up, he tells you to feel your belly. Very slowly you run your hand over it, and suddenly something kicks.

I won't bore you with all the details, but I will say that the film climaxes in a very moving scene where you give birth to your child in the middle of the Sahara Desert (don't worry, we can just shoot on a studio set filled with a bunch of sand).

Working titles are: *Another Desert Child for Raymond*, *Born Under a Desert Sun*, and *Plastic Emotions: The Story of Mr. Wonderful*.

Please contact me as soon as possible with your decision—however, I must tell you, there is no other actor that could take your place for this project. If you refuse, my brilliant screenplay will die alongside you.

Hope to hear from you soon.

ZACK STERNWALKER

P.S. As a sign of good faith, please accept this complimentary vampire.

Zack Sternwalker
P.O. Box #22883
Oakland, CA 94609

His Excellency Li Zhaoxing
Ambassador
Embassy of the People's Republic of China
2300 Connecticut Avenue NW
Washington, DC 20008

DEAR CHINA,

Let me be the first to congratulate you on your wonderful country. From what I hear, you have a lot of interesting things to look at, which brings me to the point of this letter.

The other day I was sitting around drinking beer with my mailman, Clark (he does this really funny trick where he takes out his penis, waves it around, then sticks it back in his pants).

I was lamenting about the difficulty I had getting support for my numerous creative projects when he shared an experience from his past that really got me thinking. He told me about how, when he was my age, he had attempted to start a pornographic magazine. He got together some money for a camera, found some girls who were eager to model, and thought he had a successful business on his hands.

Unfortunately the project turned out to be a bust. He was telling me that, now, in hindsight, he can see the problem was that he lacked a unique angle (as it turns out, there are many pornographic magazines to compete with, and the name he chose for his, *A Bunch of Naked Women*, just didn't stand out).

Seeing as how I'm currently broke (I recently lost my job and was forced to move back in with my mother, I decided that I might as well take my turn at the porn industry, confident that I could learn from Clark's experience and find a unique angle that had yet to be exploited.

For days I lay around the house, listening to my favorite Sammy Davis Jr. record, trying to come up with a good twist on the classic porn magazine formula (you might say that the "idea machine" had run out of gas).

At Clark's suggestion, I left the sanctity of my home (sorry, Sammy) and went to my corner liquor store, where I purchased a very large bottle of beer (I asked the clerk what kind would be best for inspiration and he insisted this brand was the very best). I walked around all night drinking, and eventually fell asleep in the bushes out front of a new apartment complex that had recently been built downtown (the mayor says that putting up expensive housing in poor neighborhoods will help revitalize the community).

The next morning I awoke to a strange sound. As I came to, I realized it was singing, and not just any singing—it was the sweet singing of Sammy Davis Jr. I walked over to the gigantic wall separating the apartments from the street and listened more closely. It seemed that someone in one of the apartments was listening to Sammy and had opened a window for the rest of the world to enjoy.

Overcome with emotion, I immediately attempted to climb the wall and find out who this mystery person was. But, despite how hard I tried, I just couldn't do it (for some reason the wall seemed to be specifically designed to keep people from scaling it).

Completely exhausted, I stared up at that great structure that had kept me from meeting a possible soulmate, and I was suddenly filled with great hate. But then, as quickly as it had come, the hatred vanished and was replaced with a strange attraction. Suddenly I saw the wall as a valiant opponent—one whose careful construction and incredible physical strength had knocked me to my knees, forcing me to stand back and admire it.

And admire it I did. In fact, after several moments I found myself becoming strangely aroused.

I was feeling both a fear and excitement I'd not felt in a long time. Following my instincts, I rose to my feet and approached the wall. I began slowly, first rubbing my fingertips against the outline of the bricks. Then, when I could hold back no further, I threw myself against it, desperately gyrating my hips and crying out in undeniable ecstasy. When it was all over, I lay on the ground completely exhausted but more satisfied than I'd felt in years.

Since my experience, I have decided that this unique fetish must be brought to the public's attention, as I'm quite confident there are others out there that share a similar passion.

As an example of my devotion, I have begun production of the first issue of my monthly adult magazine entitled *Wet Walls*, featuring beautiful photographs of the most attractive walls in town (and when I say "attractive," I don't necessarily restrict my viewpoint to some superficial notion of beauty. On the contrary, all the walls I've chosen possess a "special something" that often transcends their physical appearance).

In addition, the first issue will feature a hot new piece of erotic fiction by the acclaimed writer, Lord Reynaldo (shhhh, it's just a clever pseudonym) entitled *My First Time*.

Now here comes my big question for you.

Since this is the first issue of *Wet Walls*, I would love nothing more than if you granted me permission to photograph your highly regarded Great Wall of China for my featured spread.

Although the walls in my city are quite wonderful in their own way, I'd be lying if I said your magnificent structure didn't completely take my breath away.

And please don't worry that my photographs might cheapen or degrade your wall. As much as I love to rub up against a good hard wall (I'm only human), I still regard each one with the highest level of respect.

So far I've mapped out a fairly extensive series of shots to be taken in the late afternoon (we'll get some fantastic lighting then) as well as some at night that will be a bit more risqué (I'm going for that "business wall by day/party wall by night" theme).

As I stated before, I am a bit low on cash so if you agree to this project I'd be forced to ask you to put up the money for a plane ticket to your country (don't worry, I travel light).

Please contact me as soon as possible with your schedule of availability. Hope to hear from you soon.

ZACK STERNWALKER

P.S. As a sign of good faith, please accept this complimentary vampire.

Zack Sternwalker
P.O. Box #22883
Oakland, CA 94609

Michael J. Jordan
676 N. Michigan Ave. #293
Chicago, IL 60611

DEAR MICHAEL JORDAN,

Let me begin by admitting I'm not a basketball fan (I thought about joining the team in high school but band practice always conflicted). Despite my lack of knowledge about the game, I've heard from various sources that when it comes to getting the ball into the hoop, you're one of the very best.

Recently I've fallen on some hard times and been forced to move back in with my mom and begin the long and hard search for new employment. While all this free time has motivated me to write several brilliant screenplays (it's kind of like cooking—just a dash of this, a sprig of that, and pretty soon you have a delicious meal on your hands), it has also left me a bit bored and depressed.

To alleviate this depression, my mom—who happens to be a big fan of yours (I accidentally read her diary once and found this passage where she described making love to you in zero gravity)—suggested that I volunteer at the local community center and use my skills to help the children of our neighborhood grow into intelligent and multitalented adults.

The very next day I went down there and set up an intensive six-week screenwriting course for fourth and fifth graders.

I planned the class to meet five days a week, for six hours each day (beginning in the afternoon so as not to interfere with their normal schooling), giving them a half-hour dinner break in between the two three-hour sessions.

Much to my dismay, only one student signed up. His name is Byron Bernard.

Luckily he's very intelligent and eager to learn (he's currently working on an urban drama that focuses on a crooked blackjack dealer who goes straight and begins a brilliant career as a professional kickboxer. His working titles are: *The Fire Inside the Flame*, *Take It to the Maximum Level*, and *Byron Bernard Gets Even*).

As an added bonus, he's even volunteered to be my assistant with my various creative endeavors. But let me get back to the point of this letter.

One night as we were finishing up the screenwriting class we heard some yelling coming from the community center's gymnasium. Both of us quite curious, Byron and I ventured down the hall to see what was going on.

Apparently we had happened upon one of the community center's nighttime basketball classes, and the students seemed to be right in the middle of a slam dunk contest. As we watched in amazement, these young athletes continually slammed the ball into the hoop with so much force that the entire fixture shook.

Just as we were about to head back to the classroom, I overheard several of the young men discussing your famous basketball skills, even going so far as to insinuate that you're some kind of super being because of your ability to fly through the air on your way to the hoop.

Being someone who's always been a bit sensitive to those who spin tall tales, I immediately accused the young man of being a liar (only birds have the ability to fly).

I think this upset him because he immediately threw his basketball at me and challenged me to a fight (although I've thrown my share of punches back in grade school I generally consider myself a pacifist when it comes to these types of altercations). I told him that this would be out of the question as he's nearly half my age and I am a respected member of the adult community.

Apparently he had other plans, because no sooner had I begun to explain myself that he ran up and started punching me in the face. I fell to the ground and, despite his repeated blows, managed to coil up into my "safety ball" (this is a self-defense move I patented back in the early 80s when I was doing freelance consultation work for the Israeli army).

Although I was initially very upset that this young man had attacked me, over time I came to realize that it was just as much my fault for egging him on. Besides, I really had no grounds to call him a liar. For all I know, you really do have the ability to fly—which is why I've contacted you.

I want to put your abilities to the test. I did some research and discovered that there is a high cliff that overlooks the ocean, very near to my house. I propose that you come down sometime on a weekend (the weekdays I'm all booked up with the screenwriting class) and we head over there together. I have asked Byron to act as head cinematographer on the project (my mom has an old Super-8 he can use) and I will take on the announcing responsibilities.

My plan is to film you running at full speed towards the edge of the cliff and capture the moment when you either sail brilliantly through the air or plummet helplessly to the rocks below.

Now I realize there is some risk of physical injury involved in this project so I have contacted my doctor friend (technically he's not a doctor, but he does know a few CPR moves) and he's agreed to be present for this spectacular event.

Please contact me with your schedule of availability so we can set a firm date and gather the necessary permits from the mayor's office.

Hope to hear from you soon.

ZACK STERNWALKER

P.S. As a sign of good faith, please accept this complimentary vampire.

Zack Sternwalker
P.O. Box #22883
Oakland, CA 94609

Christian Slater
c/o David Unger International Creative Management (ICM-LA)
8942 Wilshire Blvd
Beverly Hills, CA 90211

DEAR CHRISTIAN SLATER,

Let me begin by saying that you are, without a doubt, a potentially talented actor.

Please don't be upset at my lack of enthusiasm; in fact, I feel that your abilities are really quite high. It's just that you've not been offered a project that has taken full advantage of your talent. This is why I've contacted you.

Recently I've moved back in with my mother after a very painful divorce (they say the first cut is the deepest). While this has been both good and bad for me, I have had plenty of time to nurture any and every creative seed that sprouts from my fertile brain.

The other day, while in the middle of one of my many Sammy Davis, Jr. listening sessions, our neighbor Neil knocked on the front door. He was quite apologetic for violating our privacy (he says that home should be a sacred place) but he couldn't help overhearing my record. Turns out he has been a Sammy fan for years.

Overjoyed by the discovery of a fellow aficionado, I invited him inside so we could enjoy the record together (and just so you know, this was a purely platonic gesture. Even if I did find him attractive, I'm currently dating a nice young woman who works at the local flower shop. Besides, my mother raised me with morals the size of a watermelon, and I'm not about to throw them out the window just so I can experience one moment of passion with some run-of-the-mill neighbor who just happens to have a good body).

We listened to the record, talked and generally had a good time. When he was leaving he asked me if I was familiar with the work of his favorite artist, Elton John. I said that I wasn't, so he immediately invited me over the following night to enjoy some of the recordings.

The next night, as I walked over to Neil's house, I was all jitters (this was because of my excitement about listening to a new record, not for any other reason). He greeted me at the door with a warm smile and glass of chilled champagne (he says it's the perfect beverage to accompany Elton's songs).

With time on our side, we lounged around on his gigantic leather couch, just laughing about this and that (I made a very witty comment about the similarities between champagne bubbles and the war in the Middle East). Eventually he played some of Elton John's songs, and to his excitement, I really adored them (little did I know, Neil had actually spent much of the day coordinating the song order so that I would be swept away on a magical Elton John journey).

At the end of the set, he put on a song which was supposed to deliver the final touch to his "musical cake" (he really likes when I make up funny terms like that) which was "Candle in the Wind."

Christian, let me tell you, this song really tore my heart in two. And when he told me it was written about the untimely death of Princess Diana, well, that was just too much for me to handle.

Since I was so emotional and in no state to make it home, I asked Neil if I could spend the night at his place. Luckily, he agreed (don't worry, we slept on his couch).

In the morning he cooked a wonderful breakfast (poached eggs with a delicious southwest salsa made fresh from his homegrown tomatoes) and we listened to some of the songs from the previous evening (he was careful not to play "Candle in the Wind" because he knew how intense my reaction would be).

I went home that day feeling completely rejuvenated. I sat down in front of my typewriter and couldn't stop thinking about "Candle in the Wind" and how it reminds us all of the importance of remembering the untimely deaths of people who run countries.

With this in mind, I decided to write the world's first screenplay about Princess Diana's tragic fate. And when it came time to envision the perfect leading lady, well, I immediately thought of you.

Now, I'm not stupid; I do realize you're a man. But as I stated earlier, you've never taken a role that has a real bite to it.

Please allow me to give you a brief plot treatment.

The film begins the night of Princess Diana's death. She is relaxing in her private quarters and reading a good book (something in the National Geographic vein, maybe about dolphins).

Suddenly there is a knock at her door. She rises to answer it and is overjoyed to find that it's her neighbor (and secret nighttime lover) paying her a visit. He kisses her hand and they passionately embrace, immediately tearing at each other's clothes and fondling like a couple of helpless fondlers. Aroused beyond their wildest dreams, they take their action to Princess Diana's gigantic leather couch and drink some champagne.

Then, just as they are about to begin that sacred act, we hear Elton John's "Candle in the Wind" come on the soundtrack (I'm going to add just the smallest drop of backing oboe when says the word "wind"). I envision this lovemaking scene to go on for about 90 to 100 minutes and involve various toys and jellies.

Then, just as Princess Diana and her lover are about to climax, we cut to a scene of their car exploding. As the credits roll, we play "Candle in the Wind" just one last time.

Working titles for the film are: *Thunder Street 5000*, *The Little Princess Goes to Heaven*, and *Anal Crisis IV: Immediate Backup Requested*.

If you're into this project, please let me know immediately so we can get you going on a heavy dose of female hormones (I know it's asking a lot, but just think of how much Princess Diana gave to the world, only to be scooped up prematurely by God's gigantic soup spoon).

Hope to hear from you soon.

ZACK STERNWALKER

P.S. As a sign of good faith, please accept this complimentary vampire.

Zack Sternwalker
P.O. Box #22883
Oakland, CA 94609

Oakland Police Department
455 Seventh St.
Oakland, CA 94607

DEAR THE POLICE,

Let me be the first to congratulate you on all your crime fighting. From what I hear, you guys are always driving around town arresting people.

Despite your busy schedule, I was wondering if you could do me a quick favor. Please allow me to explain.

Over the past year, I've gone through a painful divorce, lost my job, and been forced to move back in with my mom. It's taken me a while to get my confidence back, both professionally and socially.

However, I'm happy to announce that I've finally met someone who's caught my fancy. The only problem is, I don't think she's aware of my existence.

With this in mind, I decided that the best way to get her to notice me is to make her a gift that shows a bit of my creative side. At first I thought it would be a cool idea to write a screenplay about us falling in love on a Jamaican submarine, but then I decided that it'd be better to do something original.

After days spent in a creative fog (I must've listened to that Sammy Davis, Jr. record a million times) I realized that I'd never done a drawing for another person. My mind made up, I took out my pencil and paper and set right to work.

Unfortunately, I couldn't think of appropriate subject matter and sunk back into depression. The problem was, I wanted to draw the perfect thing that would get the message across that I was both creative *and* a serious lovemaker. For weeks I couldn't think of anything.

Then, one night, I awoke from a horrific dream about a unicorn that was living (rent-free) in my bedroom closet. I got up, made myself a cold glass of lemonade, and checked the closet. Of course, nothing was there (if there had been, you guys probably would've heard about it!).

As I was falling back asleep, I suddenly realized the absolute perfect thing to draw for my would-be lover that would make her realize what a great guy I am. A gun.

My creative juices flowing, I leapt out of bed and set right to work. However, when I tried to put the pencil to paper, I was unable to come up with a good mental image (as you've probably guessed, I'm not a drawer by trade).

The next day I walked over to Blockbuster (it's a store where you can pay a few dollars to borrow a movie from their large collection) and rented *Death Wish*, starring Charles Bronson. Although there were many images of guns on the screen, they were so brief that I couldn't get a good sketch down.

This is why I've contacted you. Would it be possible for me to borrow one of your guns for a couple of days? I know you guys all carry guns, so I figured you probably have a few extra lying around. I promise not to get it messed up (I won't keep it on the table during dinnertime, so don't worry) and the second I'm finished, I'll run down to the station and return it.

To show my thanks, I may be able to arrange an impromptu, officers-only concert featuring Justin Timberlake on vocals and myself on oboe (our set can get a bit loud during the more emotional tunes, so you may want to bring some earplugs).

Please let me know ASAP if you can help me out on this project, as I'm eagerly awaiting its completion (she's got me all wound up, officer). Hope to hear from you soon.

ZACK STERNWALKER

P.S. As a sign of good faith, please accept this complimentary vampire.

24 November

Dear Mr. Sternwalker,

Thank you for your letter dated 5 Oct 2004. Departmental policy does not allow us to loan weapons.

Sincerely,

Oakland Police Department
455 7th Street
Room 124
Oakland, CA 94607

Zack Sternwalker
P.O. Box #22883
Oakland, CA 94609

Microcosm Publishing
2752 N Williams Ave
Portland, OR 97227

DEAR MICROCOSM PUBLISHING,

I'd like to begin by thanking you for agreeing to publish *Please Let Me Help* by Zack Sternwalker. Although I didn't understand your reasoning at the time, I see now how the title is actually way stronger than any of my proposals.

Additionally, I wanted to apologize for subsequently sending you all 9,437 of my screenplays. I understand now that you are not a film company.

You'll be pleased to know that I followed your instructions, and after receiving my complimentary copies of *Please Let Me Help* by Zack Sternwalker, I sent along a copy to each of the celebrities and companies I'd written, congratulating them on our work together and inviting them to take a moment to pat themselves on the back.

Despite my excitement at the possibility of hearing from everyone after all these years (I told them to send an updated photo), I was a little upset when no one responded. That's when I realized that in my haste I'd foolishly neglected to include the date and time of the book release party.

As I started to write them a follow-up letter, I realized that even I didn't know the date and time of the book release party. Now, I'm not dumb, this could mean only one of two things. Either you never sent me the info about the book release party because you never intended on having one (confusing), or you were waiting for me to take the lead (more likely).

Now even though I'd love to rent out a luxurious ballroom and throw a wild party until dawn, I was thinking that this type of event called for something more low key, like a quiet get-together at my mom's house (technically I still live there too).

While I'm excited at the prospect of coming up with all the party ideas myself, I thought it'd be even more fun if a few of the guests lent a hand. Naturally, because you're a small press publisher, I thought you might like to bring down one of your printing presses (we could fit it in through the living room window), and then you, me, my mom, and the other guests could write a joint screenplay and you could print up copies at the end (don't worry, I'll map out the plot, character descriptions, sex scenes, etc.).

But if you aren't into this role (I understand not wanting to mix business and pleasure), I thought a cool alternative might be for you to stand by the door and take people's coats.

Now, don't think that I'm just going to sit back and ask you to contribute while everyone else does nothing. You'll be happy to know that after examining the talents of some of our invitees, I came up with a plan for how to put together a fantastic night of entertainment.

First off, I envision the majority of the festivities will occur in the backyard, simply because that's where we have the most space. And since music is the foundation of any successful party, I thought I'd ask Justin (Timberlake) to set up his singing equipment in the back corner (normally that's where my mom's cat exercises, but fortunately for us his unicycle is super easy to disassemble). While I'd love to give Justin free reign for the set list (he's earned it), I'm going to have to make an executive decision and insist that he stick to a list of songs that I've personally curated (and yes, they do all feature the oboe as a central instrument).

And because oboe music is typically enhanced by thought-provoking visuals, I'm asking Francis Ford Coppola (*The*

Miracle Toad, *Incubator III*, etc.) to be responsible for directing a film to accompany the songs. Since most of the tunes I've selected have an aquatic theme, I thought Francis might like to film an actual whale birth (of course, I'll let him pick the type of whale). At the film's climax, I think it'd be cool if a flock of seagulls swooped down on the remaining whale placenta and hoisted it up to reveal that it spelled out the revised title, "*Please Let Us Help*."

Naturally, this tender moment could be enhanced if we threw in some live theater. For this, I've asked Canada (French, free health care, etc.) to donate a flock of their best geese so that we could potentially release them from my mom's basement (don't worry, I'll obviously go down ahead of time and paint them to look like seagulls).

Now I'm not one for speeches, but I know that at the end of any book release party it would only be customary that I say a few words. As such I've decided to dig deep and find it within myself to explicate a little more on this collaboration and give a little insight into how it felt to grow so close with all these people and companies during our correspondence (don't worry, I'll try to keep it to under an hour).

After the guests dry their eyes, it'd be great if you took a break from printing screenplays to come outside and offer up a few poignant thoughts of your own (remember: take your time, breathe, and maintain eye contact).

Please get back to me with some possible dates and times for this special event (I'm free most nights up through the coming year). And as a sign of good faith, please accept this complimentary vampire.

ZACK STERNWALKER

I made my escape on the back of
a large giraffe. At one point I
stopped and turned around. One
of the dogs was still behind me.
I took out my gun and
blasted it. Then I continued
on.

Oakland Police: Incident Report

At 11:45pm on the night of October 5th, 2018, Officer Green was dispatched to 6507 Broadway Terrace to investigate a call about a white male, approximately 5'8", 185 lbs., who was reportedly trying to scale a wall surrounding the property of Thomas F. Cruise. Mr. Cruise, who had called police, said he had observed the suspect getting close to the top of his wall while repeatedly yelling, "Mr. Cruise, I can't get over this last part of your wall." Mr. Cruise, a local dentist who has experienced previous incidents in which people have mistaken him for the actor of the same name, immediately called the police. Upon arriving, Officer Green observed a man jump down from the wall and walk nonchalantly towards the officer's vehicle. The suspect, who was dressed in camouflage and carrying a small backpack, told the officer that he was glad the officer had arrived because he had lost his house keys and "some other stuff" on the other side of the wall. As the officer got out of his vehicle, a car suddenly pulled up and the suspect tried to jump inside. However, because the suspect moved so slowly, the officer was able to easily subdue him. The officer then instructed the driver, an older woman, also dressed in camouflage, to get out of the car and lie face down (the woman was later identified as the suspect's mother). Upon searching the suspect's backpack, the officer found a manuscript entitled, *Correspondation: A Spiritual Guide*. The suspect then explained to the officer that he had been seeking the help of Tom Cruise, the actor, to be a spokesperson for his new religious movement, but he hadn't responded to his letters. At this time, the actual resident, Thomas F. Cruise, came outside and addressed the suspect directly. Upon meeting Mr. Cruise, the suspect realized his mistake and apologized. The suspect then promised to pen an original screenplay for Mr. Cruise (the dentist) as well as for Officer Green, if they both agreed not to press charges. As the suspect was cuffed and placed inside the officer's vehicle, he called out to Mr. Cruise that the film would most likely be about a "young dentist's love affair with a married cop, resulting in the unexpected birth of a child made entirely of marijuana." The suspect was later booked and charged with criminal trespassing.

SUBSCRIBE TO EVERYTHING WE PUBLISH!

Do you love what Microcosm publishes?

Do you want us to publish more great stuff?

Would you like to receive each new title as it's published?

Subscribe as a BFF to our new titles and we'll mail them all to you as they are released!

$10-30/mo, pay what you can afford. Include your t-shirt size and your birthday for a possible surprise!

microcosmpublishing.com/bff

...AND HELP US GROW YOUR SMALL WORLD!

More books for perfectly normal weirdos: